e2

GW01087073

THE PITT

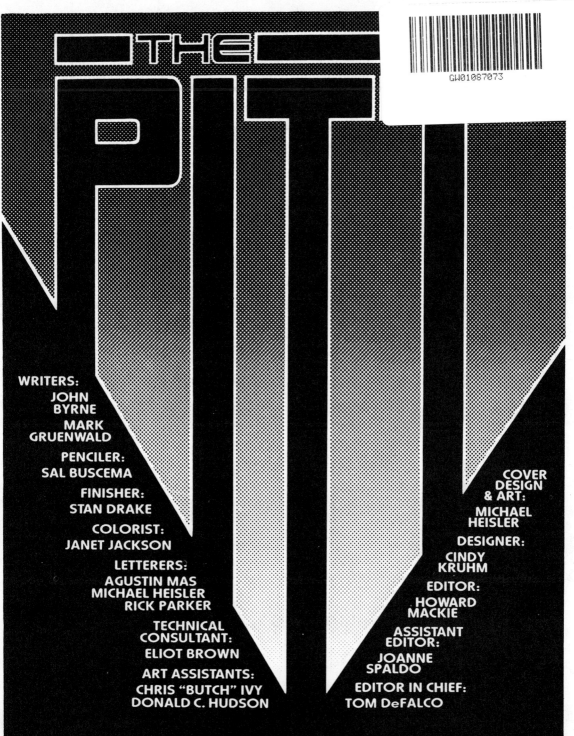

WRITERS:
JOHN BYRNE
MARK GRUENWALD

PENCILER:
SAL BUSCEMA

FINISHER:
STAN DRAKE

COLORIST:
JANET JACKSON

LETTERERS:
AGUSTIN MAS
MICHAEL HEISLER
RICK PARKER

TECHNICAL CONSULTANT:
ELIOT BROWN

ART ASSISTANTS:
CHRIS "BUTCH" IVY
DONALD C. HUDSON

COVER DESIGN & ART:
MICHAEL HEISLER

DESIGNER:
CINDY KRUHM

EDITOR:
HOWARD MACKIE

ASSISTANT EDITOR:
JOANNE SPALDO

EDITOR IN CHIEF:
TOM DeFALCO

WITNESS created by Mark Gruenwald   KEN CONNELL created by Jim Shooter
COL. MAC BROWNING created by John Byrne, Mark Gruenwald and Eliot Brown
SPITFIRE created by Eliot Brown and John Morelli

Published by Marvel Entertainment Group, Inc., a New World Company, 387 Park Avenue So., New York, NY 10016

My name is Nelson Kohler, and for the past year and a half I have been a *ghost*.

It all began two summers ago with what the media has dubbed the *White Event*. For about five seconds the sky went brilliant white all over the world. Scientists are still debating what caused it.

Whatever it was, extraordinary things began occurring in its immediate aftermath . . .

I was driving my automobile at the time. Blinded by the sudden light in the sky, I lost control of my car, crashed, and died a few hours later.

That is, my *physical form* died. My consciousness, affected by what I assume was the energy of the White Event, survived. It felt strange not to have a body, so I *imagined* myself to have one.

I've been doing it ever since. The only problem with having an imaginary body is that no one else can see me or touch me or even *hear* me. On the other hand, I have no physical limitations, and I can practically do anything I want.

I was hardly the only one affected by whatever it was unleashed by the White Event. In the days and weeks and months since, people all over the world have been developing strange paranormal forms and abilities.

I should know. For I somehow *sense* people who are in the process of becoming paranormal.

It's more than just a sensation. It's a *compulsion*. When I get that buzzing sensation in the pit of my imaginary stomach, I *have* to go and find out what's causing it. I don't know why. Maybe it's purely psychological. Maybe I'm drawn to it because it's the only thing on Earth I *can* feel.

I guess I'm like a *moth*, compelled to flit from flame to flame.

Well over a year ago, I lost count of the number of transformations I have observed. Surely it is in the hundreds by now, perhaps *thousands*.

Today, for the first time since my ethereal life began, I feel something *different* — a sensation more intense than the pain of my own *death*.

This is not the birth-cry of a lone human being in the throes of impending paranormalcy. This is more like the rape-scream of the human race itself just before the *White Event* visited its fury upon it.

Can the Great Unexplained Phenomenon be about to happen again?

I don't know. What I *do* know is that I must seek out the source of the disturbance I feel, and be there when it bursts into being.

For I am . . . the *Witness*.

I MUST TRAVERSE THE SKY *FASTER* THAN I'VE EVER GONE BEFORE--

--SOMEHOW IT FEELS LIKE THERE IS NOT MUCH *TIME* LEFT BEFORE...*IT* HAPPENS, WHATEVER *IT* IS!

WHERE AM I *HEADING?*

A *CITY* IN THE DISTANCE...*WHICH ONE?* I COULD SWOOP LOWER, READ A *ROAD SIGN.*

NO. NO TIME. BESIDES, WHAT *DIFFERENCE* DOES IT MAKE WHAT CITY'S BELOW?

STOP THAT, TIMMY!

JANEY STARTED IT!

DID NOT!

YOUR FATHER'S HAVING A HARD ENOUGH TIME DRIVING THROUGH THIS *TRAFFIC* WITHOUT YOU KIDS *ADDING* TO IT.

SORRY, DAD.

SURE WISH MR. DILLER HAD LET ME GO HOME SOONER. I KNEW TRAFFIC WOULD BE THIS BAD IF WE LEFT SO *LATE.*

AT LEAST HE GAVE YOU WEDNESDAY OFF, DEAR.

YEAH. STILL, DOUBT WE'LL GET TO *GRANDMA'S HOUSE* TILL WAY PAST THE KIDS' BEDTIME.

THE PAIN IS GETTING *LOUDER--* ITS SOURCE IS DEFINITELY SOMEWHERE IN THAT CITY AHEAD, WHATEVER IT IS.

HO-HO-HO! MERRY CHRISTMAS!

"PITTSBURGH SAVINGS AND LOAN." I MUST BE IN *PITTSBURGH, PENNSYLVANIA.*

BUT WHERE OH *WHERE* IS MY AGONY COMING FROM? SO INTENSE HERE I CAN'T QUITE *PINPOINT* IT.

I...I FEEL THE *SOURCE* OF THE DISTURBANCE *MOVING*...

...MOVING *UPWARDS,* INTO THE *SKY*...

YES, THAT MAKES *SENSE.* THAT'S *WHERE* THE WHITE EVENT *HAPPENED,* AFTER ALL.

NNGH! THE PAIN--HURTS TO EVEN *THINK*...

WHAT--? A *MAN.* A TALL BLOND MAN *FLYING--*IN NOTHING BUT HIS *UNDER-WEAR!*

IS HE-- CAN HE BE THE *SOURCE* OF THE *PSYCHIC TRAUMA* I FEEL?

HE *MUST* BE. YES, IT'S COMING FROM *HIM!*

BUT HE MUST *ALREADY* BE *PARANORMAL!* HE'S FLOATING THERE, CASUALLY DEFYING *GRAVITY!*

WHAT IS THAT HE IS *HOLDING?* A *METAL WEIGHT* OF SOME SORT? HE LOOKS LIKE HE'S ABOUT TO *SLAP* IT WITH--!

HIS *HAND.* MY GOD, THE POWER--IT'S HIS *HAND!*

OR *SOMETHING IN AND AROUND* IT--!

THE PAIN IS...*UNBEARABLE--*WHATEVER HE'S ABOUT TO DO IS *CAUSING* IT--! HE MUST BE *WARNED--STOPPED--*!

NOOOOOOOO!

I'M *TOO LATE!*

CURSE THIS *PHANTOM BODY!* THERE WAS *NEVER* ANYTHING I COULD *DO ANYWAY!*

HE'S PRESSED HIS *HAND* TO THAT METAL WEIGHT-- IT'S *GLOWING*--

NOW WHAT?!?

4

6:06 P.M. E.S.T.

WKKRAKKOOM!

WHAT WAS THAT NOISE?!? *LIGHTNING?* I'VE NEVER SEEN SUCH AN ENORMOUS STATIC DIS-CHARGE!

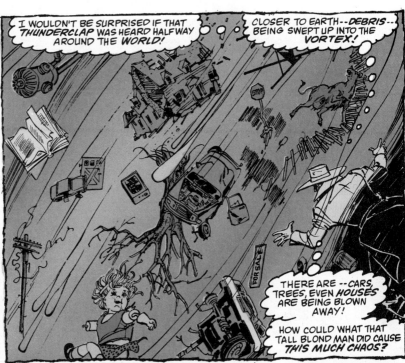

I WOULDN'T BE SURPRISED IF THAT *THUNDERCLAP* WAS HEARD HALFWAY AROUND THE *WORLD!*

CLOSER TO EARTH--*DEBRIS*--BEING SWEPT UP INTO THE *VORTEX!*

THERE ARE --CARS, TREES, EVEN *HOUSES* ARE BEING BLOWN AWAY!

HOW COULD WHAT THAT TALL BLOND MAN DID CAUSE *THIS MUCH CHAOS?*

WHAT DID HE *DO* ANYWAY? THE WIND SEEMS TO BE RUSHING *INWARD*, TOWARD THE *CENTER* OF THE EXPLOSION. THAT DOESN'T MAKE *SENSE*. I WOULD HAVE THOUGHT THAT THE AIR WOULD BE RUSHING *OUTWARD*, CARRIED BY THE *SHOCKWAVE* OF THE BLAST.

UNLESS...! COULD THE EXPLOSION HAVE BEEN SO *POWERFUL* THAT IT CAUSED A SEVERAL MILE *VACUUM?* IN THAT CASE, THE ATMOSPHERE WOULD BE RUSHING IN FROM ALL SIDES TO FILL THAT *VOID!*

THIS IS *HORRIBLE*. I SEE *BODIES* AND... *PARTS* OF BODIES HURLING BY ME-- CAUGHT IN THIS WIND!

INTANGIBLE AS I AM, THERE IS *NOT ONE THING* I CAN DO TO HELP A SINGLE SOUL! NEVER HAVE I FELT MORE... MORE *ACCURSED!*

6:08 P.M., 26 MILES AWAY...

LEONARD--WH-WHAT'S HAPPENING? THAT BLINDING *LIGHT*, THAT *EXPLOSION--* NOW THIS *WIND!* WHAT DOES IT ALL *MEAN?*

MOMMY, I'M *SCARED!*

I-I DON'T KNOW, MARGE! MAYBE--MAYBE THOSE DANGED *RUSSKIES* DROPPED THE *BIG ONE!*

YOU *THINK* SO? YOU *REALLY* THINK SO? SWEET LORD...!

DADDY, THE CAR IS *ROCKING!* I THINK IT'S GONNA *TIP OVER!*

YOU BUCKLED IN BACK THERE?

Y-YEAH!

GOOD. I--WHUHH-- WHOAHHH!

LEONNNNARRRRD!

WE'RE SPINNING-- C-CAN'T SEE WHAT---

10

6:17 P.M., GRIFFIS AIR FORCE BASE, NEW YORK...

WHAT IN THE NAME OF...??

WHATCHA GOT, SMITTY?

YOU TELL ME, GUS.

I AIN'T *NEVER* SEEN A SIGNAL LIKE THIS!

IF I'M READIN' THIS RIGHT...

PITTSBURGH JUST TURNED INTO A *CRATER*--FIFTY MILES ACROSS!

WHAT?!?

GREAT GODAMIGHTY!

HE'S *RIGHT!!* THAT'S THE ONLY WAY TO INTERPRET THAT IMAGE!

THIS IS HENDERSON AT D.C.I.

I'M DECLARING A CODE SEVEN ALERT.

GET ME THE CHIEF OF STAFF!!

6:47 P.M.

LINCOLN CRESCENT, WASHINGTON, D.C.

WHAT... WHAT *WAS* THAT...?

11

IT SOUNDED LIKE *THUNDER*...

...BUT I'VE NEVER HEARD THUNDER SO... SO *STRANGE.*

IT WAS ALMOST MORE LIKE AN *EARTH-QUAKE.* LIKE YOU FELT IT MORE THAN *HEARD* IT.

MAC...

WHAT *WAS* IT? YOU'RE WITH *SPECIAL FORCES*...YOU SHOULD *KNOW*...

I'M...NOT *SURE,* CAROL HONEY...

IT FELT LIKE SOMETHING *BIG* GOING OFF, PRETTY CLOSE BY.

BUT A *NUKE* AS BIG AS THAT WOULD FILL THE SKY WITH LIGHT, WITH SOUND, WITH *WIND*...

HEY! WHAT'S THAT *NOISE*...THAT *WIND*...

IS THAT...

NO...

MAC...!

6:51 P.M.

COLONEL BROWNING...

COLONEL MacINTYRE BROWNING, PLEASE *SHOW* YOURSELF.

THIS IS A *PRIORITY ONE* COMMAND.

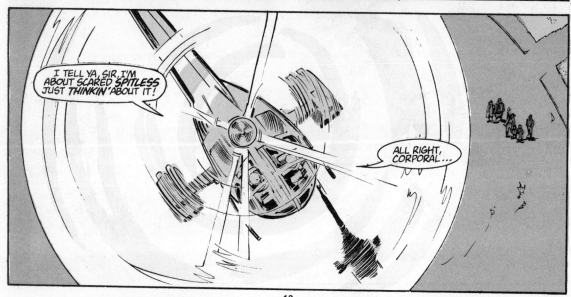

...PRESUMABLY YOU DIDN'T COME CHASING OUT TO MY HOUSE *EMPTY HANDED.*

YOU MUST HAVE SOME KIND OF *WRITTEN* ORDERS FOR ME.

B. SYNNOT

WELL, YOU CAN TAKE A LOOK AT THAT *CLIP-BOARD* ON THE SEAT BESIDE YOU, SIR.

MAYBE THAT *GOBBLEDY GOOK* WILL MAKE SENSE TO YOU!

D. BLINN

YES...

YES, IT MAKES SENSE, ALL RIGHT.

DELTA VEGA CODE. FOR USE ONLY IN CASES OF MAXIMUM DISTRESS.

LIKE IF THE *RUSSIANS* HAVE NUKED NEW YORK...

ALL RIGHT, CORPORAL,...

IF THIS INFORMATION IS *ACCURATE,* I'M ALREADY *LATE* FOR THE PARTY.

LET'S SEE WHAT THIS BABY CAN *DO.*

"I HAVE TO BE IN OHIO INSIDE TWO HOURS..."

9:01 P.M.

COMING UP ON THE OUTER PERIMETER NOW, SIR.

TAKE US UP TO FORTY THOUSAND, CAPTAIN.

I WANT THE WIDEST POSSIBLE OVERVIEW.

14

YESSIR.

BUT...SIR, I GOT THE GEIGER COUNTER RUNNIN'... ALL I GET IS NORMAL *BACKGROUND* NOISE.

SHOULDN'T THERE BE...?

DON'T ASK QUESTIONS IN A *VACUUM*, CAPTAIN.

ALL WE KNOW RIGHT NOW IS THAT THERE HAS *NEVER* BEEN AN EFFECT LIKE THIS ANYWHERE ON *EARTH* BEFORE.

WE DON'T HAVE THE *LEAST* IDEA *WHAT* TO EXPECT.

BUT, WHATEVER IT IS, IT'S SOMEWHERE *UNDERNEATH* ALL *THAT!*

I'M GOING TO TRY TO RAISE A *GROUND* STATION.

HELLO, PITTSBURGH. THIS IS COLONEL MacINTYRE BROWNING CALLING ANYONE IN THE PITTSBURGH AREA.

DO YOU COPY, PITTSBURGH?

IS *ANYONE* RECEIVING ME?

ANYONE?

SIR, WE'RE STARTIN' TO HIT SOME PRETTY *SERIOUS* BUFFETING.

WHATEVER'S GOIN' ON UNDER THAT CLOUD COVER, IT'S KICKIN' UP A HECKUVA *BREEZE*.

ALL RIGHT...

PULL BACK TO THE PERIMETER. I WANT TO RUN A FEW MORE *PASSES* AT THIS MESS...

THEN WE'RE GOING TO NEED TO HAUL IT BACK TO OPERATIONS AND START LAYING THE GROUNDWORK FOR SOME *SERIOUS* MANEUVERING.

BUT RIGHT NOW...

"I'VE GOT ONE *SPECIAL* CALL TO MAKE."

TIN LIZZIE TO *CLOSE-UP*. WE ARE RECEIVING YOU, COLONEL.

WE'RE ON THE *GO-LINE*. READY TO LAUNCH IN THREE MINUTES.

16

ATTENTION LAUNCH DECK. YOU ARE **GO** IN TWO MINUTES, THIRTY-EIGHT SECONDS.

ALL RIGHT, ALL RIGHT. KEEP YOUR **PANTS** ON, WHEELER.

C'MON, JAKE. LET'S GET 'ER **REVVED UP**...

WE HAVEN'T HAD TIME TO TEST ALL OF THE M.A.X. SUIT'S SYSTEMS SINCE THE LAST OVERHAUL.

YOU **SURE** ABOUT THIS, JEN?

WE'LL JUST HAVE TO MAKE THIS THE FIRST FULL SCALE TEST, JAKE. A LOT OF THE STUFF IN HERE HAS NEVER SEEN USE IN THE FIELD.

I'M JUST LEERY ABOUT ALL THIS. WE'VE NEVER HAD TO RUN A MISSION ON U.S. SOIL.

WHY DON'T WE TELL THE ARMY BOYS TO TAKE CARE OF THIS BUSINESS THEMSELVES?

JAKE, IN CASE YOU'VE **FORGOTTEN**, THESE DAYS WE **ARE** THE ARMY BOYS.

SPITFIRE RUNS ONLY WHEN AND WHERE UNCLE SAM SAYS.

AND IF WE WANT TO BE ABLE TO CONTINUE IN OUR **GOOD WORKS** WE HAVE TO DO WHAT UNCLE SAM WANTS.

AND TODAY, THAT MEANS CHECKING OUT WHATEVER SEEMS TO BE TAKING PLACE IN PITTSBURGH.

OKAY, LADY. YOUR SUIT.

STAND CLEAR NOW. I DON'T WANT YOU GETTING SUCKED OUT BY THE SLIPSTREAM WHEN I...

20

10:11 P.M.

KEEP IT GOING CORPORAL.

I WANT AT LEAST ANOTHER FIVE MILES COVERED BEFORE WE CALL A HALT.

YESSIR...

BUT...THE GOING AIN'T GONNA BE... *EASY*, SIR.

NO SUCH THING AS EASY IN UNIFORM, CORPORAL.

MAKE FOR THAT DIVISION OVER THERE. LOOKS LIKE FLATTER GROUND BEYOND.

OR AT LEAST LESS *DEBRIS*. SHOULD MAKE FOR SMOOTHER PASSAGE.

YESSIR.

"SMOOTHER PASSAGE," THE MAN SAYS.

HE OUGHTTA COME DOWN HERE AND SHOVEL SOMMA *THIS*.

YEAH! THEN WE'LL SEE WHAT HE THINKS ABOUT "SMOOTHER."

I'VE BEEN TRYING FOR *HOURS* TO FIND SOME POINT OF REFERENCE, SOME PREVIOUS EXPERIENCE I CAN *COMPARE* THIS TO.

BUT THERE'S *NOTHING*. NOTHING IN ANYTHING I'VE EVER SEEN BEFORE.

NO WAR DAMAGE, NO STORM DAMAGE.

AND WE'RE STILL A GOOD FIFTEEN MILES FROM THE EDGE OF...IT.

IN FACT, IT OCCURS TO ME WE'RE NOW GETTING TOO CLOSE TO MY SECURITY PERIMETER TO LET THESE GRUNTS KEEP WITH US.

CLEAN UP CREW!

FALL BACK. ONLY SECURITY G-7 BEYOND THIS POINT.

22

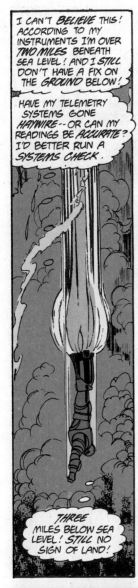

I CAN'T *BELIEVE* THIS! ACCORDING TO MY INSTRUMENTS I'M OVER *TWO MILES* BENEATH SEA LEVEL! AND I *STILL* DON'T HAVE A FIX ON THE *GROUND* BELOW!

HAVE MY TELEMETRY SYSTEMS GONE *HAYWIRE*--OR CAN MY READINGS BE *ACCURATE?* I'D BETTER RUN A *SYSTEMS CHECK.*

THREE MILES BELOW SEA LEVEL! *STILL* NO SIGN OF LAND!

SYSTEMS CHECK COMPLETE-- IT'S *NOT* AN INSTRUMENT MALFUNCTION. I REALLY *AM* THIS DEEP.

SOMEHOW THERE IS A *BIG HOLE* WHERE PITTSBURGH WAS! THE ONLY QUESTION NOW IS-- JUST *HOW BIG* IS THAT HOLE!?!

EIGHT MILES...

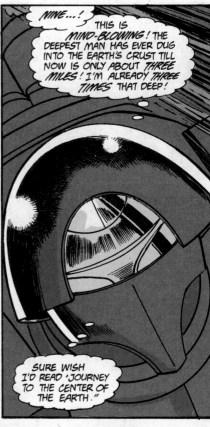

NINE...!

THIS IS *MIND-BLOWING!* THE DEEPEST MAN HAS EVER DUG INTO THE EARTH'S CRUST TILL NOW IS ONLY ABOUT *THREE MILES!* I'M ALREADY *THREE TIMES* THAT DEEP!

SURE WISH I'D READ "JOURNEY TO THE CENTER OF THE EARTH."

10:41 P.M.

FOURTEEN MILES AND STILL--*WAIT!* I AM GETTING A SOUNDING! I THINK I'VE FOUND IT--THE *BOTTOM* OF THE PIT!

BETTER CUT THRUSTERS, *LEVEL OFF* BEFORE EASING DOWN FURTHER.

CAN'T SEE A *BLINKING* THING THROUGH THIS THICK *FOG COVER!*

11:02 P.M.

A LAKE. THERE'S A *LAKE* HERE AT THE BOTTOM. HMMM... A NUMBER OF *RIVERS* RUN THROUGH PITTSBURGH--THE *ALLEGHENY* JOINS WITH-- I FORGET ITS NAME-- TO FORM THE *OHIO RIVER.* THEY MUST ALL BE *DUMPING* INTO HERE.

THAT'S NOT *ALL* THAT'S DUMPING IN. ALL THE *DEBRIS* FROM THE SURROUNDING AREA MUST HAVE BEEN SWEPT UP OVER THE EDGE...

23

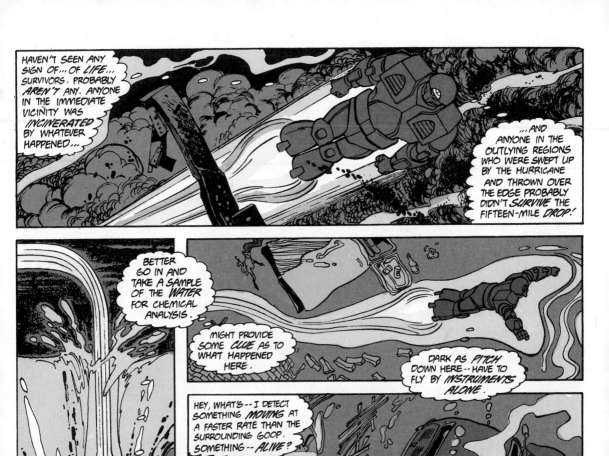

HAVEN'T SEEN ANY SIGN OF.... OF *LIFE*... SURVIVORS. PROBABLY *AREN'T* ANY. ANYONE IN THE IMMEDIATE VICINITY WAS *INCINERATED* BY WHATEVER HAPPENED...

...AND ANYONE IN THE OUTLYING REGIONS WHO WERE SWEPT UP BY THE HURRICANE AND THROWN OVER THE EDGE PROBABLY DIDN'T *SURVIVE* THE FIFTEEN-MILE *DROP!*

BETTER GO IN AND TAKE A SAMPLE OF THE *WATER* FOR CHEMICAL ANALYSIS.

MIGHT PROVIDE SOME *CLUE* AS TO WHAT HAPPENED HERE.

DARK AS *PITCH* DOWN HERE -- HAVE TO FLY BY *INSTRUMENTS* ALONE.

HEY, WHAT'S -- I DETECT SOMETHING *MOVING* AT A FASTER RATE THAN THE SURROUNDING *GOOP*. SOMETHING -- *ALIVE?*

SONAR READINGS SEEM TO MAKE IT OUT TO BE AN *AUTOMOBILE*... AN OLD *VOLKSWAGEN!* THE MOVEMENT'S COMING FROM *INSIDE!*

AAAAAAH!

LORDOHLORDOH LORDOHLORDOH--!

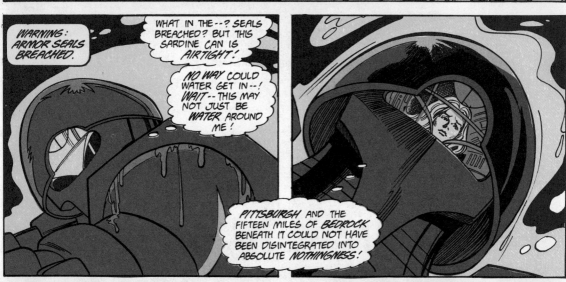

12:01 A.M., DECEMBER 23, 1987.

MADE... IT! THANK GOODNESS!

OPENED UP THE *EXHAUST VENTS* -- BUT I DON'T FEEL THE--THE *PIT-WATER* DRAINING!

DOUBT THE *AIRSEAL* ON THIS *VW* WAS ANY BETTER OFF THAN MINE.

LEONARD-- LEONARD, WHAT'S *HAPPENING?!?*

I-I DON'T *KNOW*-- WE'RE--WE'RE *BACK IN THE AIR* FEELS LIKE!

MOMMMMMMY!

SPLOOM

12:18 A.M.

WARNING: 20% IMPAIRMENT OF JET FUNCTIONS.

WHAT--?

SPT SPT SPT

OVERLOAD. OVERLOAD. REDUCE CARGO OR FURTHER IMPAIRMENT OF FUNCTIONS 99% PROBABLE.

REDUCE *CARGO*--? BUT--I--THAT MEANS I'D HAVE TO--

NO--I'M NOT GOING TO ABANDON WHAT MIGHT BE THE ONLY *SURVIVORS* OF THIS HOLOCAUST!

27

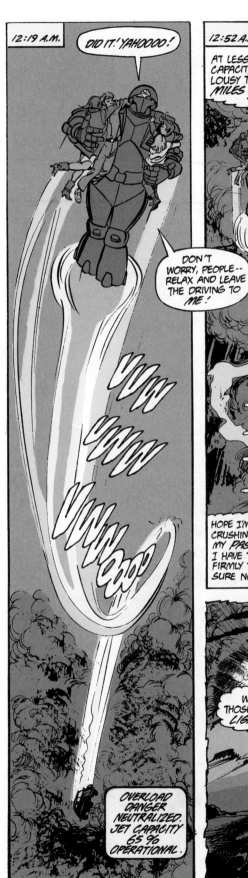

12:19 A.M.

DID IT! YAHOOOO!

DON'T WORRY, PEOPLE-- RELAX AND LEAVE THE DRIVING TO *ME!*

OVERLOAD DANGER NEUTRALIZED. JET CAPACITY 65% OPERATIONAL.

12:52 A.M. JETS ARE STILL ONLY AT LESS THAN FULL CAPACITY. I'M MAKING LOUSY TIME. STILL *FIVE MILES* OF CLIMBING TO DO!

HOPE I'M NOT CRUSHING ANY OF MY *PASSENGERS.* I HAVE TO HOLD FIRMLY TO MAKE SURE NO ONE *SLIPS.*

1:04 A.M.

THANK GOD-- THERE'S THE *EDGE* OF THE PIT! TOOK ME A BIT, BUT WE'RE *OUT.*

THERE YOU GO, FOLKS. DIDN'T I TELL YOU I'D GET YOU *OUT?* YOU'RE GOING TO BE *ALL RIGHT!*

TH-THANK YOU.

WHAT-- THOSE BRIGHT LIGHTS--!

28

RELAX! IT'S THE ARMY!

THEY'LL TAKE YOU FROM HERE--GET YOU TO SAFETY.

WOW! IT'S THAT SPITFIRE ROBOT WE WERE BRIEFED ABOUT! DIDN'T REALIZE IT WAS SO BIG!

OH, MOMMY--THAT TRANSFORMER SAVED US!

YES... IT DID, DOLLY.

BLESS YOU, WHOEVER YOU ARE. IF YOU HADN'T SHOWN UP, MY FAMILY AND I--

'S OKAY.

FOUR LIVES SAVED... I SHOULD FEEL GLAD. BUT ALL I FEEL IS NUMB THINKING OF THE MILLIONS WHO WERE VAPORIZED OR DROWNED OR BURIED--

UH, "SPITFIRE"-- COLONEL BROWNING WANTS TO SEE YOU-- ASAP.

1:29 A.M.

SIR?

YOU'RE THE ONLY ONE WHO'S SEEN THIS THING UP CLOSE, SWENSEN. I'VE READ THE TRANSCRIPT OF YOUR SIGNALS, BUT I WANT TO HEAR IT FROM YOUR OWN LIPS.

NOW.

YOU... ASK A LOT, COLONEL.

I'M NOT A SOLDIER. I DON'T PROFESS TO HAVING THE "RIGHT STUFF."

DOWN THERE IT WAS ALL I COULD DO TO KEEP FROM PUKING MY GUTS OUT.

BUT.... IF YOU WANT IT...

29

"HERE..."

"...IT..."

"...IS..."

DEAR...

...GOD...

SERGEANT...

PASS THE WORD ALONG. I WANT THIS BASE CAMP SEALED UP *TIGHT*. NO SIGNALS GO OUT UNLESS *I* SEND 'EM.

NOTHING COMES IN, BUT IT COMES IN THROUGH *ME*.

SIR.

I HOPE THAT'S NOT JUST SOME MACHO TRIP YOU'RE ON, COLONEL.

KEEP YOUR CHATTER TO YOURSELF, SWENSEN. MY ORDERS APPLY TO *YOU*, TOO.

THEN I REALLY *WILL* PUKE.

CENTRAL, THIS IS THE COMMANDER. GET ME...

"...CHEYENNE MOUNTAIN."

1:43 A.M.

YES, COLONEL.

YES, THAT'S *CLEAR*.

YOU CAN TAKE THIS AS FROM THE COMMANDER-IN-CHIEF...

YOU HAVE *MAXIMUM* AUTHORITY IN THIS.

DO *ANYTHING* YOU DEEM *NECESSARY* TO KEEP THAT AREA *SEALED.*

30

"I'LL *REPEAT* THAT, COLONEL. *ANYTHING YOU DEEM NECES-SARY*. THE PRESIDENT WILL BACK YOU *ONE HUNDRED PERCENT*."

OH, *MAN!*

TELL ME I AIN'T *SEEING* WHAT I'M SEEING.

DON'T KNOW ABOUT YOU, SMITTY.

BUT I'M SEEIN' THE *BIGGEST DANG STORY* EVER TO COME DOWN TH' PIKE. AN' I AIN'T ABOUT T'TELL *ANYBODY* IT AIN'T THERE!

BUT...

PITTSBURGH! WHERE IN THE--?

HOLD IT. SOMEBODY *CALLIN'* US...

I REPEAT: YOU ARE IN *SECURITY AIRSPACE.*

YOU ARE INSTRUCTED TO FOLLOW US BACK TO A HOLD-ING AREA. DO YOU *READ* ME, CIVILIAN CRAFT?

OH, *MAN!* THIS JUST GETS BETTER AN' *BETTER!*

YEAH, I *READ* YOU.

CAN YOU *SEE* THIS?

AFFIRMATIVE.

LOOK, BUDDY, DON'T *SCREW* AROUND.

THIS IS SERIOUS.

BUSTER, YOU DON'T KNOW THE *HALF* OF IT.

THERE'S A *STORY* DOWN THERE, AND A LITTLE THING CALLED THE *FIRST AMENDMENT* SAYS WE GOT A *RIGHT* TO REPORT IT!

OH, CRAP!

SKYWISE SIX TO GROUND ZERO.

DID YOU COPY THAT TRANSMISSION, COLONEL.

T. SHOEMAKER

AFFIRMATIVE.

YOU KNOW THE SITUATION, SKYWISE. GIVE 'EM ONE LAST WARNING...

AND... IF THEY STILL WON'T TURN BACK?

SHOOT THEM DOWN, SKYWISE.

NO! YOU...YOU CAN'T!

I HAVE THE FEELING I'M GOING TO GET VERY TIRED OF THAT PHRASE IN THE NEXT FEW HOURS.

UNDERSTAND THIS, SWENSEN: THERE IS NOTHING I CAN'T DO.

"NOTHING."

DO YOU COPY, CIVILIAN CRAFT?

THIS IS YOUR LAST WARNING. TURN BACK NOW, OR WE WILL BE FORCED TO STOP YOU.

YOU CAN'T BLUFF US, FLYBOY.

DO YOUR WORST.

...AFFIRMATIVE...

32

BDBDWOOM

2:00 A.M.

FEELS LIKE... TIME'S STANDING STILL!

STOP! YOU MUST LISTEN TO ME AND STOP THIS!

I KNOW HOW BAD YOU MUST FEEL TO HAVE YOUR LIVES SUDDENLY TAKEN FROM YOU-- BELIEVE ME. I KNOW!

DESTROYER

MONSTER

MURDERER

KILLER

GETTING AWAY

HOLD HIM

TEAR HIM APART.

BUT I HAD NOTHING TO DO WITH WHAT HAPPENED TO YOU! I SENSED SOMETHING WAS ABOUT TO HAPPEN, BUT I SWEAR TO YOU--

--THERE WAS NOTHING I COULD DO!

I'M SORRY-- TRULY, TRULY SORRY.

SWENSEN, YOU'VE BEEN SWEATING OVER THAT OVERSIZE *SOUP CAN* FOR THE PAST *TWO HOURS* WITHOUT UTTERING SO MUCH AS A WORD. NOW I KNOW KEEPING YOUR *HANDS* BUSY TAKES YOUR *MIND* OFF THE HORROR OF... WHAT YOU *SAW*--

--BUT I NEED THAT *VIDEO TRANSMISSION* YOU SAID YOU COULD PLAY ME SO I CAN DECIDE WHAT--

IT'S NOT JUST A *VIDEO-TAPE*, COLONEL. I'VE BEEN FEEDING DATA INTO *M.A.X.'S* *COMPUTER GRAPHICS* PROGRAM--

--IN ORDER TO GENERATE A *COMPOSITE IMAGE* OF THE ENTIRE PITTSBURGH AREA AS IT NOW... *EXISTS*.

RIGHT. SO WHAT'S THE ESTIMATED TIME OF COMPLETION OF THIS... *ART PROJECT* OF YOURS?

THE LAST MEGABITS OF DATA HAVE BEEN ENTERED, COLONEL. IT SHOULD ALL BE *ON SCREEN* ANY MOMENT NOW.

HMH.

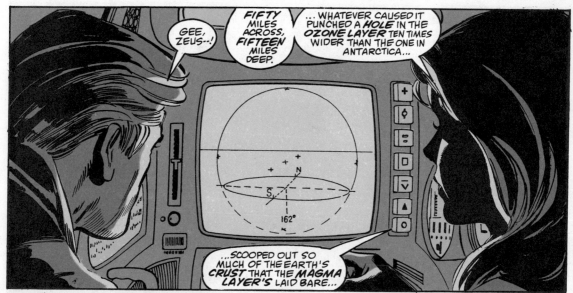

GEE, ZEUS...!

FIFTY MILES ACROSS, FIFTEEN MILES DEEP,

...WHATEVER CAUSED IT PUNCHED A *HOLE* IN THE *OZONE LAYER* TEN TIMES WIDER THAN THE ONE IN ANTARCTICA...

...SCOOPED OUT SO MUCH OF THE EARTH'S *CRUST* THAT THE *MAGMA LAYER'S* LAID BARE...

I... SEE...

YOUR SOUP CAN... IS IT *OPERATIONAL* YET? HAVE YOU FILTERED OUT WHATEVER THAT *SLUDGE* YOU TOLD ME SEEPED IN?

I SUPPOSE SO.

GOOD. I NEED YOU TO GO BACK *IN THERE...* GATHER MORE *DATA* FOR THE SCIENCE BOYS...

THAT COMPUTER DIAGRAM YOU SHOWED ME *SPOOKS* ME. THIS AREA SEEMS VERY *UNSTABLE*... I CAN'T IMAGINE WHAT THE IMPACT ON THE ENVIRONMENT IS GOING TO BE... WE'LL NEED MORE *DATA*... *MUCH* MORE...

SIR, THERE MAY BE MORE *SURVIVORS* IN THE AREA,

MAYBE NOT IN THE... THE *CRATER*, BUT ALONG THE *EDGE*, IN THE OUTLYING *AREA*, PEOPLE WHOSE *HOUSES* COLLAPSED ON TOP OF THEM... CAUGHT UNDER *DEBRIS*... BLEEDING FROM BROKEN *GLASS*...

I WANT TO USE THE *SPITFIRE* SUIT TO *SEARCH* FOR THEM. THE DEVASTATED AREA IS SO *BIG*, SO *INACCESSIBLE*, NO ONE ELSE WILL BE ABLE TO *REACH* THEM IN TIME...!

NOBLE SENTIMENTS...

...BUT I CATEGORICALLY *FORBID* IT!

37

38

39

4:21 A.M.

THE CITY'S *GONE*... NOTHING LEFT BUT A *HUGE CRATER* RAPIDLY FILLING WITH WATER AND DEBRIS.

IT'S HORRIBLE. THE MIND CAN'T ACCEPT SUCH...SUCH *CARNAGE*, SUCH *LOSS OF LIFE*.

MY MIND COULDN'T. I JUST COULDN'T BRING MYSELF TO ACKNOWLEDGE THE *REALITY* OF WHAT HAPPENED...

I WENT *INSANE*. I BEGAN TO HALLUCINATE A SCENARIO FAR EASIER FOR ME TO ACCEPT THAN THE DEATHS OF *A MILLION PEOPLE!*

I IMAGINED *SURVIVORS*--PHANTASMAL BEINGS LIKE *MYSELF*...BEINGS WHO BLAMED ME FOR WHAT HAPPENED TO THEM.

WHY? WHY DID I IMAGINE THEM *BLAMING ME?* THERE WAS NOTHING *I* COULD HAVE DONE TO STOP THE TALL BLOND MAN. I'M JUST A *STUPID GHOST*, FOR GOD'S SAKE!

I HAVEN'T BEEN ABLE TO DO *ONE BLESSED THING* FOR WELL OVER A YEAR NOW.

I CAN'T *AFFECT* ANYTHING-- I'M JUST A *WITNESS!* AND A VERY *POOR ONE* AT THAT, DISREGARDING THE EVIDENCE OF WHAT PASSES FOR MY *SENSES* FOR SOME NONSENSE OUT OF THE *TWILIGHT ZONE*.

I ONLY WISH-- WHAT'S THAT *SOUND?*

WHHNNNNN

41

WHAT POSSESSED ME TO *HIDE?* I MAY *NEVER KNOW* WHAT IT WAS NOW.

GUESS IT DOESN'T *MATTER,* ALL THAT MATTERS IS THAT I FIGURE OUT WHAT TO DO *NEXT...* SOMETHING *MEANINGFUL.*

NO ONE KNOWS WHY THEY WERE PLACED ON EARTH... OR WHY THINGS HAPPEN TO THEM AS THEY DID. IT'S SOMETHING A PERSON HAS TO *FIGURE OUT* FOR HIMSELF, GIVEN ENOUGH *TIME...*

THERE WAS *NO REASON* WHY I WAS DRAWN TO PITTSBURGH AND MADE TO LIVE THROUGH WHAT I HAVE. NONE AT ALL-- UNLESS I *MAKE A* REASON.

AND BY THE *POWER* THAT MAKES ME WHAT I AM, I *KNOW* WHAT I'M GOING TO DO. I AM GOING TO *FIND* THE TALL BLOND MAN AND MAKE CERTAIN HE'S *DEAD.*

AND IF HE'S *NOT,* I WILL NOT REST UNTIL I FIND A WAY TO MAKE HIM *PAY.* PITTSBURGH--YOU *SHALL BE AVENGED!*

4:57 A.M.

I SHOULD BE *DOING* SOMETHING. I'M A SOLDIER, AN OFFICER-- I SHOULD BE LEADING MY TROOPS AGAINST THE *ENEMY.*

BUT WHO'S THE *ENEMY* HERE? WHO WILL TAKE *RESPONSIBILITY* FOR THIS? WHO CAN WE PIT OUR MIGHT AGAINST TO SET THE WORD *RIGHT* AGAIN?

EXCUSE ME, COLONEL, THERE'S SOMETHING COMING OVER THE AIR THAT YOU SHOULD SEE.

HMM?

THAT NEWS SHOW, *NIGHTLINE...*

THEY'VE ALREADY FIGURED OUT *SOMETHING'S* GOING ON?

YOU MIGHT SAY THAT, SIR.

-- VIET AUTHORITIES HAVE JUST TRANSMITTED *INFRARED PHOTOGRAPHS* OF THE EASTERN UNITED STATES TAKEN BY SOVIET "WEATHER SATELLITES" WHICH *SHOW* THE AREA AROUND *PITTSBURGH, PENNSYLVANIA* TO HAVE BEEN TOTALLY *LEVELLED...*

PENTAGON OFFICIALS COULD NOT BE REACHED TO *CONFIRM* OR *DENY* THESE PHOTOGRAPHS. PITTSBURGH HAS BEEN TOTALLY *BLACKED-OUT* TO TELECOMMUNICATIONS SINCE ABOUT SIX O'CLOCK LAST NIGHT...

THE NEWS GOT OUT. DESPITE EVERYTHING I'VE DONE...*THE NEWS GOT OUT!*

THAT CIVILIAN COPTER I HAD SHOT DOWN... THERE WAS *NO NEED.*

LOUSY RUSSIANS! PROBABLY WANTED TO BE THE FIRST TO SPREAD THE WORD SO *THEY* WOULDN'T GET *BLAMED...*

YOU *HAVE?* I'LL TELL HIM!

COLONEL, SKYWISE HAS GOT *SPITFIRE* IN HER SIGHTS! THEY WANT TO KNOW IF THEY SHOULD *OPEN FIRE.*

NO.

TELL SKYWISE TO HOLD FIRE.

ENOUGH DAMAGE HAS BEEN DONE FOR ONE DAY.

6:06 A.M. E.S.T.

DAWN... THE COLOR OF BLOOD AND RUST...

LAST NIGHT I TOLD SOMEONE WE'RE LOOKING AT A WHOLE NEW *BALLGAME* HERE. YEAH... ONE WHERE THE *OLD RULES* DON'T APPLY... WHERE THE *BALL-PARK* HAS BEEN TURNED INSIDE OUT... WHERE NEITHER THE PLAYERS NOR THE SPECTATORS KNOW THE *SCORE*...

I'M *TIRED.* I'D BETTER GO WRITE UP MY *REPORT.*

'Twas three days before Christmas and all though the town, not a creature was stirring, because they were all *dead*.

(No, too *flippant*. Let's start again.)

My name is *MacIntyre Browning* and I'm a bird colonel in the Army's Defense Intelligence Agency. I've seen a lot of disturbing things in my day — in Southeast Asia, in Grenada, in El Salvador. But what I saw in Pittsburgh last night blows everything else away.

(Too *matter-of-fact*. This is what I get for trying to express myself after going without sleep for two days. One more time.)

Yesterday the world as we knew it came to an end. It didn't end with a bang exactly, nor did it end with a whimper. But it ended with at least one million people dead or dying. With a hundred towns and villages destroyed. With the earth bleeding from a mortal wound.

God only knows how or why it happened. The *"Pittsburgh Effect,"* like the so-called *"White Event"* a year and a half ago, are phenomena without precedent, beyond the realm of *known science*. Someone suggested that the so-called "super hero" who turned up in Pittsburgh may have had something to do with this. I'm betting we're *never* going to know.

(I've got it. I'm on a roll now.)

Pittsburgh is *gone*. Completely. This fact must be understood *absolutely*. The city was within a sphere of earth and atmosphere measuring fifty miles in diameter which was completely converted into the strange, inert material now at the bottom of the crater — the *Pitt*, as I've heard it ghoulishly referred to. Our chances of analyzing a pure sample of this material were destroyed by the storms and influx of debris that followed the Effect. Not to mention the waters of the Monongahela and Allegheny Rivers which are pouring over the rim, creating the world's most spectacular water falls and adding to the substance at the bottom.

So the world ended yesterday when Pittsburgh did. Not with a bang, not with a whimper, but with one million unanswered questions. We are left with ruptured *tectonic plates*, a hotbed of *volcanic activity*, and a *hole* in the ozone layer so big I'm going to make out a check to skin cancer research the first chance I get. We're left with a planet that's a whole different place from what it was when we all went to sleep in our safe, snug beds two nights ago.

Merry Christmas, world.

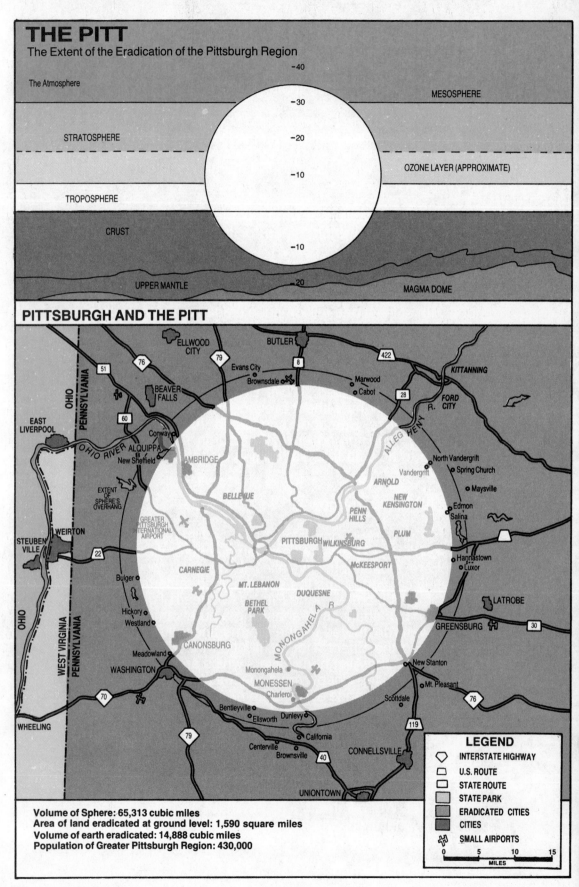

THE PITT
The Extent of the Eradication of the Pittsburgh Region

The Atmosphere

MESOSPHERE

STRATOSPHERE

OZONE LAYER (APPROXIMATE)

TROPOSPHERE

CRUST

UPPER MANTLE

MAGMA DOME

-40
-30
-20
-10
-10
-20

PITTSBURGH AND THE PITT

ELLWOOD CITY
BUTLER
KITTANNING
Evans City
Brownsdale
Marwood
Cabot
BEAVER FALLS
FORD CITY
EAST LIVERPOOL
Conway
North Vandergrift
Spring Church
ALQUIPPA
Vandergrift
New Sheffield
AMBRIDGE
ARNOLD
Maysville
NEW KENSINGTON
Edmon
Salina
BELLEVUE
PENN HILLS
PLUM
STEUBEN VILLE
WEIRTON
GREATER PITTSBURGH INTERNATIONAL AIRPORT
PITTSBURGH
WILKINSBURG
Hannastown
Luxor
EXTENT OF SPHERE'S OVERHANG
CARNEGIE
McKEESPORT
LATROBE
Bulger
MT. LEBANON
DUQUESNE
GREENSBURG
Hickory
BETHEL PARK
Westland
CANONSBURG
Meadowland
New Stanton
WASHINGTON
Monongahela
Mt. Pleasant
MONESSEN
Charleroi
Scottdale
Bentleyville
Ellsworth
Dunlevy
WHEELING
California
Centerville
Brownsville
CONNELLSVILLE
UNIONTOWN

OHIO
PENNSYLVANIA
OHIO RIVER
WEST VIRGINIA
PENNSYLVANIA
OHIO
MONONGAHELA R
ALLEGHENY
R.

LEGEND
◇ INTERSTATE HIGHWAY
▢ U.S. ROUTE
▭ STATE ROUTE
▨ STATE PARK
▨ ERADICATED CITIES
▨ CITIES
✈ SMALL AIRPORTS

Volume of Sphere: 65,313 cubic miles
Area of land eradicated at ground level: 1,590 square miles
Volume of earth eradicated: 14,888 cubic miles
Population of Greater Pittsburgh Region: 430,000

0   5   10   15
MILES